LOONEY TUNES ™

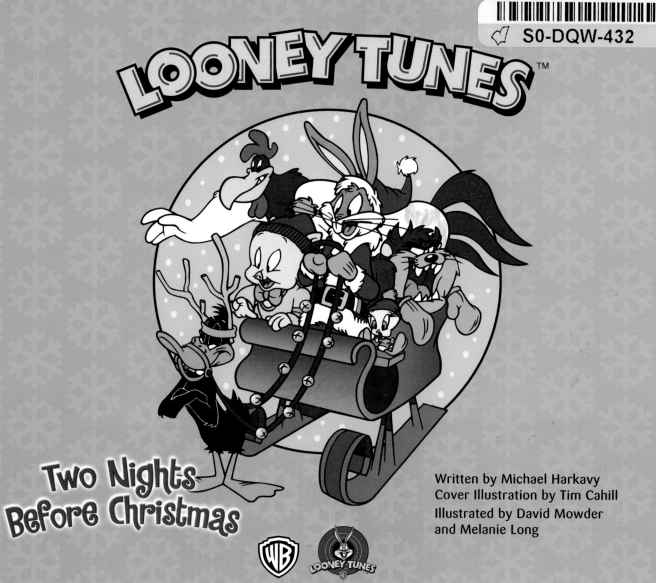

Two Nights Before Christmas

Written by Michael Harkavy
Cover Illustration by Tim Cahill
Illustrated by David Mowder
and Melanie Long

Dalmatian Press, LLC, 2005. All rights reserved. Printed in the U.S.A.
The DALMATIAN PRESS name, logo and spotted spine are trademarks of Dalmatian Press, LLC, Franklin, Tennessee 37067.
No part of this book may be reproduced or copied in any form without written permission from the copyright owner.

ISBN: 1-40371-580-7 (X) 1-40371-884-9 (M)

05 06 07 08 LBM 10 9 8 7 6 5 4 3 2 1
14377 Looney Tunes: Two Nights Before Christmas

'Twas two nights before Christmas, and all through the house,
Looney Tunes were a-stirring ("Andele!" yelled the mouse).

The stockings were hung by the chimney with care;
Daffy's was biggest, though he wouldn't share.

And everyone lay wide awake in his bed
(Dewusions of gwandeur danced in Elmer's head).
And Granny in her curlers, with Sylvester on her lap,
Both hoped that St. Nick had remembered his map.

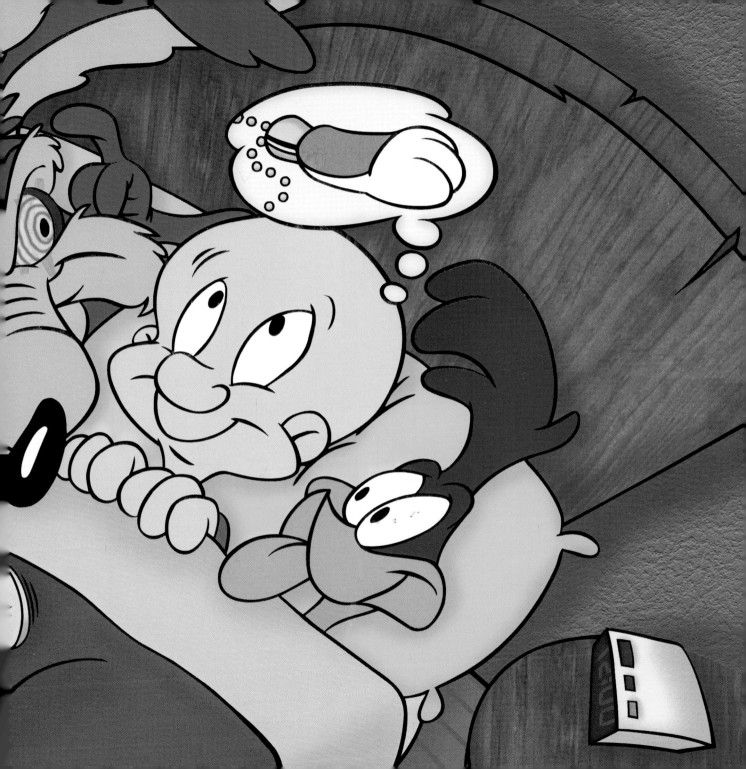

When out on the lawn there arose such a clatter,
That they all sat up straight to see what was the matter.

Away to the window they flew like a flash,
Tore open the shutter (then Taz ate the sash).

Yosemite Sam on the roof in the snow
Gave neighbors a reason to say, "Uh-oh."

When what to their wide open eyes should appear
But a sleigh packed with gifts . . . and not a single reindeer.
The driver was sneezing and coughing, quite sick.
"Omigosh!" they all shouted. "It's sniffly St. Nick!"

As slow as molasses he inched down the flue,
With a "Snort!" and a "Snuffle!" a "Wheeze!" and "Ah-choo!"
"Roll call!" he sputtered. "Don't whine or argue!
Now, Porky! Now, Foghorn! Now, Pepe Le Pew!

"My reindeer are sleeping, my elves are on strike,
Mrs. Claus is so cranky, she said 'Take a hike!'
So I took out my sleigh and rode off with a sniff;
Now I need all your help to deliver these gifts!"

The Looney Tunes knew the old boy was in trouble—
So they turned on their heels and took off on the double!
When he caught them he twinkled, his dimples grew merry!
He gave each a noogie that glowed like a cherry.

He spoke not a word and went straight to his work.
He harnessed, he strapped, and secured with a jerk.

Then he sprang to his sleigh and he gave a deep sigh,
As Foghorn called out, "Ah-say, chickens can't fly!"
But like magic they lifted, they flew and they swirled,
And brought Christmas joy to the rest of the world.

So gifts were delivered in a bit of a hoax—
Happy Christmas to all, and to all...

That's all, folks!